Dear Parent:

Congratulations! Your child is taking the first steps on an exciting journey. The destination? Independent reading!

STEP INTO READING® will help your child get there. The program offers five steps to reading success. Each step includes fun stories and colorful art. There are also Step into Reading Sticker Books, Step into Reading Math Readers, Step into Reading Write-In Readers, Step into Reading Phonics Readers, and Step into Reading Phonics First Steps! Boxed Sets—a complete literacy program with something for every child.

Learning to Read, Step by Step!

Ready to Read   Preschool–Kindergarten
• big type and easy words • rhyme and rhythm • picture clues
For children who know the alphabet and are eager to begin reading.

Reading with Help   Preschool–Grade 1
• basic vocabulary • short sentences • simple stories
For children who recognize familiar words and sound out new words with help.

Reading on Your Own   Grades 1–3
• engaging characters • easy-to-follow plots • popular topics
For children who are ready to read on their own.

Reading Paragraphs   Grades 2–3
• challenging vocabulary • short paragraphs • exciting stories
For newly independent readers who read simple sentences with confidence.

Ready for Chapters   Grades 2–4
• chapters • longer paragraphs • full-color art
For children who want to take the plunge into chapter books but still like colorful pictures.

STEP INTO READING® is designed to give every child a successful reading experience. The grade levels are only guides. Children can progress through the steps at their own speed, developing confidence in their reading, no matter what their grade. Remember, a lifetime love of reading starts with a single step!

Thomas the Tank Engine & Friends™

CREATED BY BRITT ALLCROFT

Based on The Railway Series by The Reverend W Awdry.
© 2009 Gullane (Thomas) LLC.
Thomas the Tank Engine & Friends and Thomas & Friends are trademarks of Gullane (Thomas)
Limited.

HIT and the HIT Entertainment logo are trademarks of HIT Entertainment Limited.

Visit us on the Web!

www.stepintoreading.com

www.thomasandfriends.com

Educators and librarians, for a variety of teaching tools, visit us at
www.randomhouse.com/teachers

Library of Congress Cataloging-in-Publication Data
Stuck in the mud / based on The railway series by the Reverend W. Awdry ; illustrated by
Richard Courtney.
   p. cm. — (Step into reading. Step 1)
"Thomas the Tank Engine & Friends."
ISBN 978-0-375-86177-2 (trade) — ISBN 978-0-375-96177-9 (lib. bdg.)
I. Awdry, W. II. Courtney, Richard. III. Thomas the tank engine and friends.
PZ7.S937563 2009   [E]—dc22   2009010028

Printed in the United States of America
20 19 18

HIT entertainment

THOMAS & FRIENDS™

Stuck in the Mud

Based on The Railway Series
by the Reverend W Awdry

Illustrated by Richard Courtney

Random House 🏠 New York

Click-clack!

Click-clack!

Thomas puffs
down the track.

Thomas finds
an old engine.

Hiro is broken.

Will he be sent
to the scrap yard?

No!

Thomas will fix him.

Uh-oh!

Here comes Spencer!

"I'm going to tell!"
says Spencer.

Oh, no!

Hiro needs help!

Thomas puffs off
to get help.

Click-clack!

Click-clack!

Thomas and Spencer
race down the track.

Splat!

Spencer falls

into the mud!

Now Thomas must help
<u>two</u> engines.

He tells Sir Topham Hatt.

Clang! Clang!
Bang! Bang!
Hiro is fixed.

25

But who will

help Spencer?

Thomas is too small.

Hiro will.

He huffs and puffs.

He pulls Spencer
out of the mud.

"Thank you,"
says Spencer.

Hooray for Hiro!

Click-clack!

Click-clack!

All the friends steam

down the track.